For my dear and helpful daughters
Abigail, Jennifer, and Amanda
(and special thanks to
Ann D. and Amy E.)

First published 1995 by Walker Books Ltd
87 Vauxhall Walk, London SE11 5HJ

10 9 8 7 6 5 4 3 2 1

© 1995 Marylin Hafner

This book has been typeset in Bembo.

Printed in Hong Kong

British Library Cataloguing in Publication Data
A catalogue record for this book is available
from the British Library.

ISBN 0-7445-4008-9

MUMS DON'T GET SICK!

Marylin Hafner

WALKER BOOKS
AND SUBSIDIARIES
LONDON • BOSTON • SYDNEY

Saturday was a special day at Abby's house. She didn't have to rush to school, and Mum and Dad were not at work.

But this Saturday when Abby woke up, something seemed different.

Abby went into Mum's room.

Then she got dressed and went downstairs.

After breakfast, Dad had to go to the shops.

YOU CAN STAY IN YOUR PLAYPEN WHILE I DO MY WORK.

I'LL PICK SOME FLOWERS FOR MUM'S ROOM.

A FEW LEAVES WOULD BE GOOD.

THOSE SHOULD CHEER HER UP!

Next, Abby put a wash on.

Sarah came to the door.

Abby managed to get the wet clothes
into the dryer … but David was soaking
and the floor was flooded.

She put David into dry clothes.

OH, DAD,

EVERYTHING IS A MESS!

I BROKE A BOWL AND DAVID ATE ALL THE BISCUITS AND THE WASHING MACHINE OVERFLOWED AND THE JELLY WON'T SET AND I CAN'T TURN OFF THE DRYER.

Dad heated Mum's special soup and Abby made ham sandwiches for lunch.

Then they all went upstairs to help Mum get ready for lunch.